The Gifts
of Wali Dad

The Gifts of Wali Dad

A TALE OF INDIA AND PAKISTAN

Retold by Aaron Shepard

Pictures by Daniel San Souci

5362

Atheneum Books for Young Readers

ABOUT THE STORY

This is a retelling of "Story of Wali Dâd the Simple-hearted," found in Andrew Lang's *Brown Fairy Book* (1904). About his own source Lang says only that the story was told to a Major Campbell "by an Indian."

The dominant influences of this story are Islamic and Zoroastrian rather than Hindu. This suggests a likely origin in India's northwest. Since Pakistan has now split off from that corner, I have thought it best to attribute the tale to both countries.

Wali Dad rhymes with "Wally Todd." *Paisa*, the smallest Indian coin, is pronounced PAY-suh. *Khaistan* is pronounced KI-ston. *Nekabad* is pronounced NEK-kuh-bod. *Peri* is pronounced PEH-ree.

Peris are an import into India from Persian mythology. Originally considered evil, their image changed gradually to benevolent beings akin to fairies or angels. It is said they feed only on the odor of perfume.

Atheneum Books for Young Readers. An imprint of Simon & Schuster Children's Publishing Division, 1230 Avenue of the Americas, New York, New York 10020.   First edition.
10 9 8 7 6 5 4 3 2 . 1   Printed in the United States of America.

Library of Congress Cataloging-in-Publication Data.

Shepard, Aaron.   The gifts of Wali Dad : a tale of India and Pakistan / retold by Aaron Shepard ; pictures by Daniel San Souci. — 1st ed.   p.   cm.   Summary: An Indian/Pakistani folktale in which an impoverished grass-cutter finds that gifts can be a mixed blessing.
ISBN 0-684-19445-7 [1. Fairy tales. 2. Folklore—India. 3. Folklore—Pakistan.] I. San Souci, Daniel, ill. II. Title. PZ8.S3425Gi 1995   398.2'0954'07—dc20   [E]
94-14175

For my mother, Lillian
—A. S.

For Seth Robert Diamond,
the newest member of the family
—D. S. S.

In a little hut far from town lived an old grass-cutter named Wali Dad.

Every morning Wali Dad cut and bundled tall, wild grass. Every afternoon he sold it as fodder in the marketplace.

Each day he earned thirty paisa. Ten of the small coins went for food. Ten went for other needs. And ten he saved in a clay pot under his bed.

In this manner Wali Dad lived happily for many years.

One evening Wali Dad dragged out the pot to see how much money it held. He was amazed to find that his coins had filled it to the brim.

"What am I to do with all this money?" he said to himself. "I need nothing more than I have."

Wali Dad thought and thought. At last he had an idea.

The next day Wali Dad loaded the money into a sack and carried it to a jeweler in the marketplace. He exchanged all his coins for a lovely gold bracelet.

Then Wali Dad visited the home of a traveling merchant.

"Tell me," said Wali Dad, "in all the world, who is the noblest lady?"

"Without doubt," said the merchant, "it is the young queen of Khaistan. I often visit her palace, just three days' journey to the east."

"Do me a kindness," said Wali Dad. "The next time you pass that way, give her this little bracelet, with my compliments."

The merchant was astonished, but he agreed to do what the ragged grass-cutter asked.

Soon after, the merchant found himself at the palace of the queen of Khaistan. He presented the bracelet to her as a gift from Wali Dad.

"How lovely!" she said, admiring the bracelet. "Your friend must accept a gift in return. My servants will load a camel with the finest silks."

When the merchant arrived back home, he brought the silks to the hut of Wali Dad.

"Oh, no!" said the grass-cutter. "This is worse than before! What am I to do with such finery?"

"Perhaps," said the merchant, "you could give it to someone else."

Wali Dad thought for a moment. "Tell me," he said, "in all the world, who is the noblest man?"

"That is simple," said the merchant. "It is the young king of Nekabad. His palace, too, I often visit, just three days' journey to the west."

"Then do me another kindness," begged Wali Dad. "On your next trip there, give him these silks, with my compliments."

The merchant was amused, but he agreed. On his next journey he presented the silks to the king of Nekabad.

"A splendid gift!" said the king, admiring the silks. "In return, your friend must have twelve of my finest horses."

So the merchant brought the king's horses to Wali Dad.

"This grows worse and worse!" declared the old man. "What could
I do with twelve horses?"

But after a moment Wali Dad said, "I know who should have such a gift. I beg you, keep two horses for yourself, and take the rest to the queen of Khaistan!"

The merchant thought this was very funny, but he consented. On his next visit to the queen's palace, he gave her the horses.

Now the queen was perplexed. She whispered to her prime minister, "Why does this Wali Dad persist in sending gifts? I have never even heard of him!"

The prime minister said, "Why don't you discourage him? Send him a gift so rich, he can never hope to match it."

So in return for the ten horses from Wali Dad, the queen sent back twenty mules loaded with silver.

When the merchant and mules arrived back at the hut, Wali Dad groaned. "What have I done to deserve this? Friend, spare an old man! Keep two mules and their silver for yourself, and take the rest to the king of Nekabad!"

The merchant was getting uneasy, but he could not refuse such a generous offer. So not long after, he found himself presenting the silver-laden mules to the king of Nekabad.

The king, too, was perplexed and asked his prime minister for advice.

"Perhaps this Wali Dad seeks to prove himself your better," said the prime minister. "Why not send him a gift he can never surpass?"

So the king sent back twenty camels, twenty horses with golden bridles and stirrups, twenty elephants with golden seats mounted on their backs, and twenty liveried servants to care for them all.

When the merchant guided the servants and animals to Wali Dad's hut, the grass-cutter was beside himself. "Will bad fortune never end? Please, do not stop for a minute! Keep for yourself two of each animal, and take the rest to the queen of Khaistan!"

"How can I go to her again?" protested the merchant. But Wali Dad pleaded so hard, the merchant consented to go just once more.

This time, the queen was stunned by the magnificence of Wali Dad's gift. She turned again to her prime minister.

"Clearly," said the prime minister, "the man wishes to marry you. Since his gifts are so fine, perhaps you should meet him!"

The next morning Wali Dad rose before dawn. "Good-bye, old hut," he said. "I will never see you again."

The old grass-cutter started down the road. But he had not gone far when he heard a voice.

"Where are you going, Wali Dad?"

He turned and saw two radiant ladies. He knew at once they were peris from Paradise.

Wali Dad sank to his knees and cried, "I am a stupid old man. Let me go my way. I cannot face my shame!"

"No shame can come to such as you," said one of the peris. "Though your clothes are poor, in your heart you are a king."

The peri touched him on the shoulder. To his amazement he saw his rags turn to fine clothes. A jeweled turban sat on his head. His rusty scythe was now a polished cane.

So the queen ordered a great caravan made ready, with countless horses, camels, and elephants. With the trembling merchant as guide, she and her court set out to visit the great Wali Dad.

On the third day the caravan made camp, and the queen sent the merchant ahead to tell Wali Dad of her coming.

When Wali Dad heard the merchant's news, his head sank to his hands. "Oh, no!" he moaned. "Now I will be paid for all my foolishness. I have brought shame on myself, on you, and on the queen. What are we to do?"

"I fear we can do nothing!" said the merchant, and he headed back to the caravan.

"Return, Wali Dad," said the other peri. "All is as it should be."

Wali Dad looked behind him. Where his hut had stood, a splendid palace sparkled in the rising sun. In shock he turned to the peris, but they had vanished.

Wali Dad hurried back along the road. As he entered the palace, the guards gave a salute. Servants bowed to him, then rushed here and there, preparing for the visitors.

Wali Dad wandered through countless rooms, gaping at riches beyond his imagining. Suddenly, three servants ran up.

"A caravan from the east!" announced the first.

"No," said the second, "a caravan from the west!"

"No," said the third, "caravans from both east and west!"

The bewildered Wali Dad rushed outside to see two caravans halt before the palace. Coming from the east was a queen in a jeweled litter. Coming from the west was a king on a fine horse.

Wali Dad hurried to the queen.

"My dear Wali Dad, we meet at last," said the queen of Khaistan. "But who is that magnificent king?"

"I believe it is the king of Nekabad, Your Majesty," said Wali Dad. "Please excuse me for a moment."

He rushed over to the king.

"My dear Wali Dad, I had to meet the giver of such fine gifts," said the king of Nekabad. "But who is that splendid queen?"

"The queen of Khaistan, Your Majesty," said Wali Dad with a smile. "Please come and meet her."

And so the king of Nekabad met the queen of Khaistan, and the two fell instantly in love. A few days later their marriage took place in the palace of Wali Dad. And the celebration went on for many days.

At last Wali Dad had said good-bye to all his guests. The very next morning he rose before dawn, crept quietly from the palace, and started down the road.

But he had not gone far when he heard a voice.

"Where are you going, Wali Dad?"

He turned and saw the two peris. Again he sank to his knees.

"Did I not tell you I am a stupid old man? I should be glad for what I have received, but . . ."

"Say no more," said the other peri. "You shall have your heart's desire." And she touched him again.

So Wali Dad became once more a grass-cutter, living happily in his hut for the rest of his days. And though he often thought warmly of his friends the king and queen, he was careful never to send them another gift.